There's a HAMSTER in my Pocket!

To Jean B. Campbell

First published in Great Britain in 2011 by
Frances Lincoln Children's Books, 4 Torriano Mews,
Torriano Avenue, London NW5 2RZ
www.franceslincoln.com

A catalogue record for this book is available from the British Library.

ISBN 978-1-84780-118-0

Set in Plantin

Printed and bound by CPI Group (UK) Ltd, Croydon, CR0 4YY in May 2012

3 5 7 9 8 6 4

There's a HAMSTER in my Pocket!

Franzeska G. Ewart

Illustrated by Helen Bate

F

FRANCES LINCOLN
CHILDREN'S BOOKS

Beset with Worries

I must be a Born Worrier.

Don't get me wrong – I can go for ages without a care in the world, but there are times when I'm simply *beset* with worries. And last summer was one of those times.

'Beset with worries', by the way, is an expression I got from my best friend Kylie Teasdale. Kylie's dead set on being a writer when she grows up, and she has this little notebook where she writes down good words and phrases.

She let me look at it once, and I found 'beset with worries' on the 'B' page, underneath 'bravado' and 'bucolic'.

There were three worries besetting me last summer. The first one, which had a Worry Factor of 10, was the family business, Farooq's Fruits.

The second one, with a Worry Factor of 8.5, was Auntie Shabnam from Lahore.

The third one, which only had a Worry Factor of 4, making it more of an Annoyance than a Worry, was Kylie's Russian Dwarf hamsters.

Of all the Worries, Farooq's Fruits was far and away the worst. It was the Mother Of All Worries.

It began one night, when I tiptoed downstairs for a glass of water and heard Mum and Dad talking in the living room. Something about their voices made me stop and listen.

They were talking about the shop, and they were using words like 'recession' and 'falling profit margins'. Dad kept sighing, and Mum kept saying she was sure it would be all right, in a voice that clearly meant she wasn't.

By this time my ear was almost bonded to the living room door, so when Dad gave his biggest sigh yet and said, "And then there's the business of the health and safety inspection . . ." I heard every word, clear as a bell.

I didn't entirely understand what 'recession' and 'falling profit margins' were, but I knew they were *not* good news, and I understood perfectly how serious a failed health and safety inspection was. The next day, though, when I asked Mum and Dad if anything was wrong, they just smiled and said of *course* not.

They couldn't fool me, though. Not for a minute. And when I asked Kylie what 'recession' meant, and she told me it was 'a period of general economic decline', I felt absolutely sick.

So that was the First Worry, and it was, as I discovered at breakfast the next morning, the direct cause of the Second Worry.

"Auntie Shabnam is coming to stay for a while," Dad announced. "All the way from Lahore. Exciting, isn't it?"

We were all sitting round the table. Nani was eating soggy Weetabix and Bilal, who had just cut his second tooth, was gnawing the handle of his mug.

The news completely floored us. For a while, no one spoke.

"Auntie Shabnam has agreed to help boost the business," Dad went on. "Give us advice, and so forth."

"Very sharp, my sister is," Mum put in. "Brimful of business acumen."

I turned to ask Nani what 'business acumen' was, but she was glaring down into her spoonful of mushy cereal as though it contained all the sins of the world. I decided I could wait.

Dad cleared his throat and looked directly at me.

"Your mum and I have decided, Yosser," he said, "that Auntie Shabnam would be most comfortable in Nani's room. We're going to convert it into an executive office for her."

A sound like a small, wet, explosion came from Nani's direction. Dad ignored it.

"So Nani will move in with you," he went on.

I swear I heard my stomach go *splat!* as it hit the kitchen floor.

"It's only for a short while," Dad added, apologetically.

"And it'll give us a chance to give Nani's room a nice, fresh lick of paint," Mum said, very brightly. "And declutter it."

At the word 'declutter', Nani's nostrils flared. She glowered over at Dad, then at Mum, then finally at me.

I glowered back. I was beyond words.

Mum didn't seem to notice all the bad vibes coming from Nani and me, though. She went on talking about decluttering, and painting and wallpapering, as if it was some kind of treat.

And all the while, I was picturing my little room with Nani's bed in it, and Nani's hundreds of bottles of cough linctus and nerve tonic and indigestion medicine, and her thousands of tubs of foot powder and face powder and tooth powder, and her corn plasters.

I pictured my neat shelves covered with her stuffed birds and bats and lizards, and my walls hung with her butterfly and moth collection, and every last bit of my carpet littered with her big vests, and I badly wanted to cry.

"As Shahid says, it's only for a couple of months," Mum told Nani. "Then you can move back. And think of all the extra space you'll have when we clear out a few things . . ."

Nani's nostrils flared wider than ever. She banged the table with her fist, sending Bilal an eyeful of wet Weetabix. He began to howl.

"Not one thing will you clear out," Nani hissed through clenched teeth. "Not one single, solitary thing, as I live and breathe." Then she rammed her spoon hard into her mouth, and didn't say another word till bedtime.

So that was Worries one and two. And, in the

light of *them*, Worry Number three hardly seems worth mentioning.

Worry Number three concerned Kylie.

Now, I don't think I'm a jealous person. I try not to be, anyway. But that summer I was really jealous of Kylie. And the reason was Kylie's pets.

Kylie's *menagerie*.

I would have loved a pet. I'd pleaded for a dog, but Mum and Dad said that was out of the question because Nani couldn't take it for walks during the day while the rest of us were out.

I'd begged for a cat, but they said Nani was allergic – though how anyone who's lived all their life surrounded by stuffed leopards and lynxes could possibly be allergic to a mere *cat* is beyond me.

Eventually I'd had to settle for a goldfish.

It was a really nice goldfish, with big black eyes and a frilly tail, and I kept it in a bowl on the shelf above my bed and called it Smartypants.

I liked watching Smartypants, and feeding him and so on, but what I really wanted was something I could cuddle.

Kylie, on the other hand, was *tripping over* things to

cuddle – what with her dad's dozens of ferrets, and her mum's seven (yes, *seven*) Papillon dogs, and her brother's white rat, Fang.

And now, as if that wasn't enough, they'd only gone and given her a pair of hamsters.

Russian Dwarf hamsters, to be precise. The cutest, cuddliest animals you ever saw, with little brown stripy bodies and little white tummies and furry little feet and bright little eyes like shiny black pinheads.

"I'm calling them Toffee 'n' Caramel," Kylie told me when she took me up to her room to see them. "'Cause they're s-o-o-o-o sweet."

And, boy, were Toffee 'n' Caramel ever sweet! Kylie and I played with them all the time. We loved letting them crawl up our sleeves and sniff our necks and dive down under our jumpers and out again. They were drop-dead gorgeous!

I didn't begrudge Kylie Toffee 'n' Caramel one bit, and she was great at sharing them with me. But no matter how hard I tried not to be, I was still jealous.

That summer, it seemed to me that Kylie had everything going for her. But, as it turned out, Kylie had a big worry too. Kylie had Sniper.

Sniper

The evening after the 'Auntie Shabnam' news broke, Kylie and me were in her bedroom building a castle for Toffee 'n' Caramel, and that was when she told me about Sniper.

Castle Hamster was amazing. We'd collected loads of old washing-up liquid bottles and toilet roll insides, and we'd glued them onto a big cardboard box to make turrets and secret tunnels.

Then we'd painted the whole thing bright pink and added sparkly detail with glitter pens and red love-heart stickers. It looked quite magical.

Kylie was trying to get a cardboard flag to stick straight up from the battlements, and she was getting more and more frustrated because it kept keeling over. Suddenly she said, “My mum’s forty next week. Which is old, Yosser, really old.”

I held the flag while she fixed it with more Sellotape. “That’s great, Kylie,” I said. “Your mum loves parties – and there’s sure to be a *humungous* one.”

Kylie nodded. “We’re having a surprise fancy-dress party for her the night before, ‘cause her birthday’s on Sunday,” she said. “It’s in the Masons’ Arms and Dad says no expense has been spared.”

She stuck the last bit of Sellotape on, and sat back. The flag was still wonky. She looked over at me, and for a moment I thought she was going to cry. When she spoke again, the words came out in a rush.

“I’m worried Sniper’s going to ruin it all,” she said. “He’s been in loads of trouble this summer, him and his mates. He won’t do anything Mum and Dad say, and the other week the police came round and they had a long talk. Then they issued him with a warning.”

She took a deep breath. Her bottom lip was trembling.

“He’s said some terrible things to Mum and Dad, Yosser,” she went on, very quietly. “He’s been like a different person these past few months.”

I was horrified. Everyone knew that Dean 'Sniper' Teasdale was a bit wild, but I thought he was cool. In fact, Sniper was another thing I envied Kylie. *I'd* have liked a big brother with Heavy Metal T-shirts and a ring in his nose. I'd have swopped Sniper for Bilal any day.

"Mum's beside herself with worry," Kylie went on. "You can tell, because she's spending hours and hours in her vegetable patch. She can't think beyond her potatoes and her carrots and her purple-leafed broccoli . . ."

Kylie sighed. "It's not healthy, Yosser," she said. "It's like she's in denial."

I stuck a big bit of Blu-tack on the flag so that it didn't dare go wonky again, and then I crawled over to Kylie and put my arm round her.

"I'm sure Sniper wouldn't do anything to spoil your mum's special birthday," I said. "He's just going through a difficult phase."

Then, hoping to cheer her up, I asked, "What are you going to get her?"

It had the opposite effect. Kylie sighed again.

"I don't know," she said. "I can't seem to get my head round the present. I think it's because I'm so worried about everything else."

I gave her another squeeze. Then I went over to the hamster cage and lifted Toffee 'n' Caramel out.

"Come on, Your Majesties," I said, in as jolly a voice

as I could muster. "Allow me to transport you to your royal residence."

I put them down outside the portcullis (which we'd drawn on in silver pen), pulled on a piece of string to raise it, and pushed their bottoms till they slid inside. Then I lowered the portcullis and left them to settle in.

"I'll help you find the perfect present for your mum," I told Kylie. "Something really pretty."

Kylie looked a bit better then, and when one of the royal hamsters popped its head up and peered over the pink battlements, she cheered right up.

"I was thinking of a jewellery box," she said. "One lined with red velvet that plays music and has a ballerina going round. Only I'm kind of strapped for cash."

Then her voice changed. "I was wondering. . ." she said, and then she bit her lip.

I thought she was going to ask me for a loan, because she sounded like I do when I'm after something, and I was getting ready to tell her I was sorry but *I* was pretty much broke too, when she went on.

". . . if you'd help me spy on Sniper?"

I was dumbfounded. "Spy on him?" I said. "Isn't that a bit extreme?"

Kylie took hold of my shoulders and looked right into my face. I could see from the expression in her eyes and the way her hair stuck up even more than usual that she was deadly serious.

"They're plotting something, Yosser, him and his mates," she said. "I've seen them creeping into the house, carrying stuff."

"What kind of stuff?" I asked, but Kylie shrugged.

"I never get a proper look," she said, "because it's always dark. But some of it's massive. . ."

Suddenly I had the most terrible picture in my head of Sniper and his mates, Germane and Twista, with their heads down and their hoods up, creeping through the darkness with big sacks on their backs.

Sacks full of horrible, suspicious-looking things for committing horrible, dastardly crimes. . .

That evening, I'd been hoping to tell Kylie my own worries about Auntie Shabnam and the decluttering of Nani's room, but now *my* worries flew right out of the window. Compared to Kylie's, they were peanuts.

Just then, we heard a dull thud from outside.

"It's them," hissed Kylie. "The gang. Turn off the light!" and she crawled over to the window.

Taking care to keep my head down, I did what I was told and together we stared out into the street.

There they were, creeping up the garden path – Sniper, Germane and Twista. A cold shiver ran up my back, because they looked exactly, precisely as I'd imagined they would. Their heads were down, their hoods were up, and Germane and Twista were carrying a long, pointed object that looked like a fat spear.

Sniper led the way, and he was clutching a bag to his chest. Ugly-looking metal objects were sticking out of it. He opened the door and he and Twista went in.

There was a clatter and a lot of *shushing*, and then they emerged, empty-handed. Taking the bag from Germane, Sniper muttered, "OK guys, see ya. And don't forget the mallet."

Kylie and me stopped breathing. 'The mallet' sounded absolutely terrible, but what we heard next was infinitely worse.

"Get a big heavy one, mind," Sniper told Germane urgently. "So we just need one bang. . ."

Germane nudged Twista, and they both laughed. "We know wot you is saying, man," Germane assured Sniper.

"We got just da job," Twista added. Then he and Germane jumped off the path onto the lawn and launched into a rap routine.

Kylie and me watched and listened in awed silence. That rap struck dread into our hearts.

"Big an' heavy wif a metal head," Twista sang.

"Bang-bang-bang, an' it'll knock 'em dead!"

"Bang-bang-bang," Germane continued, "it is an awesome sound,

"Bang-bang-bang and they go into da ground. . . Yay!"

With a series of loud whoops, Sniper joined them and they all danced wildly round Kylie's mum's prize rose bush, till Kylie's dad banged on the window and told them to give over and act their age.

As Germane and Twista disappeared into the shadows, and the words of their rap echoed eerily down the street, I reached for Kylie's hand and gave it the hardest squeeze possible.

The box from Samarkand

Next day, the Decluttering began.

We started by clearing Nani's shelves. I stood on a ladder and handed things down to Mum, who put them carefully into labelled boxes. Nani stood grimly behind Mum, watching her like a hawk, and Bilal sat in the smallest box, gnawing it to a pulp.

One of the boxes was labelled 'For throwing out', and every time Mum put something into it, Nani gave an enormous *tut* and picked it back out again. By lunchtime, the 'For throwing out' box contained two used corn plasters, three sweetie wrappers and a toothpick, and Nani had a face like a smouldering volcano.

I was in a bad mood too, because I badly wanted to be with Kylie. No matter how hard I tried, I just couldn't get my head round what had happened the night before.

After Germane and Twista had left, Kylie and I had sat frozen at the window, thinking about the terrible Mallet Rap we had just heard.

"It sounds bad, Kylie," I said, though actually I thought it sounded a great deal worse.

It was ages before Kylie spoke. "We need to find out what they're planning," she said at last, "and stop them before someone gets hurt."

"Surely your mum's seen something," I said. "Like, when she's gone into Sniper's room to do the hoovering. . ."

But Kylie shook her head. "Sniper's got a *Do not enter on pain of death* notice stuck to his door," she said. "No one dares."

A terrible picture flashed through my mind then of Sniper standing behind his bedroom door with a crowbar, waiting to bludgeon anyone who dared enter. I wanted to stay and start the spying right away, but it was already way past my bedtime.

As we went downstairs, Kylie pointed out Sniper's bedroom door. Under the *Do not enter on pain of death* message, he'd drawn a skull and crossbones *and* a hangman's noose.

I shuddered. Sniper was certainly taking no chances. . .

***

It was late in the morning when I made my Discovery. Mum was downstairs fixing lunch, Bilal was fast asleep in a mound of damp cardboard shavings, and Nani was sitting all hunched up on the stairs. I'd just packed a stuffed porcupine and climbed back up to check that the shelf was empty, when I saw it, right in the corner, covered in cobwebs and dust. It was a carved wooden box.

I lifted it down and wiped it, and that's when I saw just how beautiful it was. It was shaped like a cube, and there were flowers carved all over it. The petals of the flowers were carved into patterns, too, with pale, pinkish-white pearls that looked like the inside of shells.

I sat beside Nani and put the box in her lap. "Where did you get it, Nani-jee?" I said.

For a while Nani glowered down at the box. Then she picked it up, spat on it, and wiped it hard with the corner of her dupatta. The clean bit glowed fiery red, and now I could see that the whole surface was covered with delicate, swirly lines. They curved this way and that round the pearls, and they looked as though they were made of pure gold.

Neither of us moved when Mum called us for lunch. Nani kept glowering, and I kept looking at her, wondering why on earth she wasn't pleased. If it had been *my* long-lost box, I'd have been pleased as anything.

Then the most surprising thing happened. With a snort of annoyance, Nani handed it back to me.

“Put it in the ‘For throwing out’ box, Yosser,” she said. “I don’t want it.”

And she heaved herself up and thumped her way downstairs.

I was flabbergasted, but I also couldn't believe my luck. If Nani really didn't want the box, perhaps she'd let *me* have it, then Kylie could give it to her mum. It would be the perfect fortieth birthday present. Perhaps it even had red velvet inside.

I pulled it and twisted the top, but it wouldn't open, so I put it in my pocket, brushed the cardboard pulp off Bilal's head and took him downstairs to join Mum and Nani at the table.

I was dying to ask Nani more about the box, but I decided I'd wait till we were alone. It was obvious Nani had major issues with it.

In the afternoon Mum went to the shop, leaving us to drag the boxes into my room and unpack them. Now the decluttering was over, and Nani had won, she cheered up, and quite enjoyed telling me exactly where she wanted everything put.

I'd tried to persuade her to leave a few of the animals in their boxes, but she was having none of it. And as I filled my shelves with desert rats and wild cats and armadillos and bats, I felt more and more miserable.

I was worried about Smartypants too. I'm not sure how well goldfishes can see things that aren't in the water, but there was a wildcat right beside his bowl, and he kept swimming up to it, and opening and closing his mouth as though he was screaming for help.

It was quite distressing. Goldfish bowls magnify things, so the wildcat probably looked like an enormous sabre-toothed tiger to Smartypants. In the end, I found a large box of Elastoplast and put it between him and the wildcat to act as a sort of barrier. I wasn't at all sure it helped, though.

When the last box was empty, Nani and me sat down and looked around. Even without her bed, there was hardly a square centimetre of space.

Nani nudged me hard with her shoulder. "Cheer up, Yosser," she said. "We'll be all right, you and me and the fish. You'll see."

I gave a brave smile, but I didn't feel it. The reality of the situation had fully kicked in now, sending my Auntie Shabnam Worry Factor soaring to a spectacular 9.2. After a few nights with Nani, I suspected it could rise even higher.

I took the beautiful box out of my pocket. "How do you get it to open?" I asked.

Nani frowned. "You won't ever get it to open," she said, "because it's a puzzle box, and the key's long lost."

"What's a puzzle box, Nani-jee?" I asked.

Nani took off her glasses, shut one eye, and examined the box up close. Very, very carefully, she placed her fingertips on three of the pearl petals and gave a sharp twist. All of a sudden the sides of the box sprang out, and I saw that there was a heart-shaped hole right in its middle.

"Wow!" I said. "*Now* will it open?"

But Nani had lost interest. Shaking her head, she began to search for Bilal.

"The key's a wooden heart," she said. "It fits into the hole. But like I said," she added, as she hauled him out from under a pile of bubble-wrap, "it's long lost."

Dragging Bilal by the hand, she headed for the door. Then she stopped and stood, chewing the inside of her lip, which is what she does when she's thinking hard.

"The box was a gift," she said at last, "from someone I once knew, who journeyed to Samarkand."

A little thrill ran up my back. Journeying to Samarkand sounded incredibly romantic and mysterious.

"Let's not throw it out, Nani-jee," I said, hugging the box to my chest. "It's too beautiful to throw out. . ."

"Keep it if you like," Nani said with a shrug. "Just don't show it to me again." And she stomped off.

I gave the box another wipe and put it in my underwear drawer. Later, I decided, I'd clean it up properly, and search for the heart-shaped key. Then Kylie could have it for her mum.

I couldn't wait to see Kylie's face when she saw the gold patterns and the carved flowers. Even if the box didn't play a tune or have red velvet and a ballerina, it was a lot nicer than anything she could buy. It wouldn't help her stop worrying about Sniper, but at least it would be *one* problem solved.

But I didn't give Kylie the beautiful box after all. I kept it hidden away in my underwear drawer.

I kept it hidden because, that night, something happened that made me go off that box in a Very Big Way.

Unimaginable Horrors

After tea, Kylie and me took our minds off Sniper by building an extension to Castle Hamster, and inventing a game.

The extension was a maze made of old vacuum cleaner tubing. It started at the portcullis and snaked round and round Kylie's bedroom.

We stuck yoghurt pots at various points in the maze to make blind alleys, and put numbers on them and food inside. The game was to place bets on which hamster would turn up where. Kylie was score-keeper.

Toffee had just run into Tub Number Four for the third time, putting me well in the lead, when the front door slammed. Kylie leapt up and peeped out.

"Sniper's gone," she hissed. "Quick!" And without even waiting to write down the score, she led the way to his room.

We stood for a while under the *Do not enter on pain of death* notice, listening. From inside, we could hear weird, eerie music, and every now and then a muffled scream.

"He's left a DVD on," Kylie whispered. "He won't be out for long. One of us needs to keep a lookout."

I went and hung over the banister while Kylie slipped in. After a while, she came back out looking absolutely shell-shocked.

"Well?" I said. "Did you find anything out?"

Kylie shook her head. "You need to see that room, Yosser," she said. "It defies description."

I took a look inside, and I shook my head too. I've seen some terrible rooms in my time, but Sniper's was something else.

The ceiling was black. The walls – what you could see of them – were black. The curtains, which were drawn across and fastened with clothes pegs, were black. There were posters with skulls and swords and blood on them, and everywhere, from floor to ceiling, lay bags, and boxes, and gigantic shapes covered in black plastic.

"Can't I put the light on?" I asked, but Kylie shook her head again.

"Sniper only uses candles," she said. "He's saving the planet."

Then she gave me a little push. "He'll be back any minute," she said. "Go and search for clues. And don't worry if you hear scuffling – it'll just be Fang."

Arms outstretched, I shuffled my way into Sniper's room. The air was smoky and made my eyes water, and the only light came from a computer screen. It was really hard to make anything out.

I *had* to find something out, though. I had to know what that terrible rap was all about. Most of all, I had to know who was going to be bang-bang-banged with a mallet before they *were*.

I took a deep breath and ran my hand up and down one of the black plastic shapes, trying to work out what might be inside. It felt like a bundle of pointed stakes, with nails sticking out. I shuddered.

In one corner of the room, there was a little pool of bluish light from the computer screen. I squeezed my way round, opened one of the plastic bags, and peered inside. I could just make out a smooth, rounded handle, but I couldn't tell what was at the top.

A dagger? An axe?

Suddenly a bloodcurdling scream rang out from the computer, and I swung round. When I saw the picture on the screen, my whole body froze in utter horror. It was a man's face, and I have never, in my entire life, seen anything as scary.

His skin was pale, pale grey, and seemed to be made up of little squares that were stuck on with pins. His eyes were pale too, and unbelievably evil-looking, and there were wormy things coming out of his mouth. It was *gross*.

He was standing on a box or something, screaming

down at a woman, and she was screaming up at him. Then he jumped down and started to walk towards the woman, and part of me didn't want to see what he was going to do to her, and part of me just had to.

I heard Kylie shouting, "Sniper's back!" but I couldn't stop watching. I just couldn't.

The woman was smiling now – an odd, cunning sort of smile – and she was walking slowly towards the man with the pins. She was holding something in her hand. The camera zoomed in for a close-up, and when I saw what it was, I swear my heart stopped beating.

It was a box. A carved, wooden box.

Kylie was beside me now, tugging desperately at my arm, but my eyes were glued to the screen. The woman was twiddling at the box, and it was changing shape, just like Nani's box from Samarkand. Now it wasn't a cube any more – it had bits sticking up at the corners, and it was glowing.

She was holding it up to the man with the pins, and both of them were screaming as if there was no tomorrow.

"Come on, Yosser!" Kylie shouted. "Come *on*!"

But I didn't. At that moment, not even the thought of being bludgeoned to death by Sniper could have moved me away from that computer screen.

Then our very worst nightmare happened. Heavy footsteps thundered up the stairs, and the bedroom

door flew open. The woman on the computer scream gave one last bloodcurdling shriek, and the bedroom filled with an overpowering smell of fish and chips.

Kylie and me clung together and backed against the wall. There, in the lighted doorway, was the enormous, hooded shadow of Sniper Teasdale. He had a fish tea in one hand, and a little bundle in the other. The little bundle was moving.

"Wot is you doin' in my room?" Sniper snarled. He indicated the 'keep out' notice with his head. "Can you not *read*?"

Kylie began to edge towards the door.

"We heard your computer," she said. "We knew you'd want it turned off. . ."

"Eats up energy," I added, still with one eye on the screen, where the man with the pins seemed to be melting. "Increases your carbon footprint like nobody's business. . ."

With a grunt, Sniper dumped the fish tea on top of the computer and picked up a box of matches. He held the moving bundle to his chest and tried to open the box. All the matches fell out.

"No one," he growled, "comes into my room without my *express* permission."

He glared over at Kylie. "Specially *you*," he added.

Then he pushed the little bundle into my arms, picked up the matches and lit a black, skull-shaped candle.

The bundle gave a whimper. Then it gave a distinct meow. In the candlelight I could just make out ginger-and-white stripes and a pink nose and a set of little white whiskers.

I don't know what came over me, but all of a sudden I had the most overwhelming need for something to cuddle. And I heard myself say, "Can I have it, please?"

Sniper sank to the floor in front of the computer, turned the volume up, and opened his fish tea.

"Sure you can 'ave it," he said. "It's name's Killer Queen. Belongs to Germane," he added, through a mouthful of haddock, "but 'is mum says 'e can't keep it. An' neither can I, on account of Fang."

It was the longest sentence I'd ever heard Sniper say, and it made waves of excitement zing up my back.

My own kitten. My very own cute, cuddle-able kitten!

Kylie was gesticulating wildly from the door and in a daze I sidled over to join her. I thanked Sniper, who muttered, "OK, now *git*," and, gratefully, Kylie and me did.

In the safety of Kylie's room, we examined Killer Queen.

She was tiny. Her ears were flat and her eyes were only just open. She nestled into my neck and made little sucking noises. Then she began to purr.

My head was spinning. All I could do was hold her close.

Kylie leant against me and stroked her little stripy head with one finger.

"What about your gran's cat allergy?" she asked softly.

I could feel Killer Queen's heart beating against my neck, and I had to clench my teeth to stop from crying.

"I'm keeping her," I said very firmly. "I'm definitely keeping her."

I walked home with Killer Queen under my sweatshirt. She kept pumping her paws up and down and sucking at my tummy, and it was the most comforting feeling in the world.

And after the horrors I'd seen that evening, I sure as anything needed some comforting.

Nightmare

When I got home, Mum was in the kitchen, making naan.

They'd shifted Nani's bed into my room that evening, she told me. It had been quite a struggle, and it was an extremely tight squeeze. Now, Nani was so exhausted she was having an early night.

"Your nightie's on the door handle," Mum said. "Be careful when you climb over her," she added.

She wiped the flour off her hands and took hold of my chin. Closing one eye, she examined my face.

"Are you all right?" she asked. "You look peaky, and there's a funny smell. . ."

She pulled my right eyelid up, peered into my eye, then did the same with my left eyelid. I prayed that Killer Queen wouldn't make a noise.

Then Mum noticed the bulge. "Are you constipated?" she said, glaring down at it.

"Just a bit," I said. "But basically I'm fine. . ."

Mum, however, was not convinced. "Stick out your tongue," she ordered.

I was absolutely terrified now. If the kitten started to squirm, I was done for.

Sticking my tongue out as far as it would go, I backed away towards the door. With a determined look, Mum followed me, and I was sure I was in for the full abdominal examination.

Thankfully, however, she changed her mind and decided to go with her initial diagnosis. She gave me a cup of milk, stuck four dates onto the saucer, and told me to go to bed immediately. Massively relieved, I made my escape.

I reckoned there was only one place to hide Killer Queen, and that was Nani's room, so I crept in. It was empty, apart from a small pile of boxes in the corner.

I sat on the windowsill in the dark and ate the dates. Then I poured some milk into the saucer, and watched Killer Queen lap it up. After three saucerfuls, she clambered shakily onto my lap and fell asleep.

There was a good view of Kylie's house from Nani's bedroom window. The light was still on in Kylie's bedroom, and I pictured her snuggling under her pink 'Princess' duvet, worrying herself sick about her mum and Sniper.

Then I looked along to Sniper's room. His windows were deadly black, and I thought about his bags and boxes with their terrible contents, and the dreadful man with the pins in his head, and the box.

The puzzle box that looked so much like Nani's box from Samarkand. . .

My stomach was churning badly now, and the last thing I wanted to do was to go to bed and lie in the dark, listening to Nani snoring, but I knew I had to. I took off my sweatshirt, laid it inside one of the boxes, and put Killer Queen on top. Then I tiptoed out.

I clambered over Nani, avoiding her bulgier bits, and I lay, wide-awake in the half-light, watching Smartypants swimming round and round, peering round the

Elastoplast box at the wildcat's gaping jaws. I don't think I've ever felt so scared or so miserable.

Then the weirdest thing happened. The room began to glow, and through a misty haze I saw Smartypants swimming nearer and nearer, till he was floating right in front of me, like a big frilly orange balloon.

His big black eyes sparkled dazzlingly bright, and then, suddenly, they weren't big and black any more. In fact, they weren't Smartypants's eyes any more. They were small and pale, and they smouldered with evil.

They belonged to the man with the pins in his head.

This close, I could see every pin and every flap of skin on his face. I could also see that he was clutching something in his hand, and I knew it was the puzzle box.

I tried to scream, but no sound came out. I tried to move, but it was as though I was stuck fast to the bed.

It was such a helpless feeling. I knew that Nani was lying right there beside me, but I couldn't speak to her or even touch her. I was paralysed with fear.

Then the man with the pins spoke. "Beware the Curse," he told me in a gravelly whisper. "Beware the Curse of Samarkand!"

I heard a clicking noise and I saw a light, so I knew he'd opened the box. Then I felt him pressing down on me, and the glow from the box got brighter and brighter till it hurt my eyes.

"Look inside," the pin man said, with an evil laugh. "*Dare* to look inside. . ."

I couldn't, though. I shut my eyes tight, and all the time the light was getting brighter, and the terrible box was getting closer.

The laughter was getting louder too, because now there wasn't just the pin man floating above my bed, there was Sniper too. His face, underneath a gigantic grey hood, pushed up in front of the pin man, and he waved an enormous mallet at me.

"Open the box," Sniper chanted. "Open the box, or I'll bang-bang-bang you wif me mallet. . ."

He raised the mallet high in the air and as he did, the weight on my chest got so heavy, I could hardly breathe. I managed to make a little whimpering noise, and that made Sniper shout at me again.

This time, however, he seemed to have forgotten all about the box.

"Where's me cough linctus, Yosser?" he roared down at me. "Where have they put me cough linctus?"

With one great jump I woke up. I was drenched in sweat, and my arms were flailing about. There was Nani sitting astride me, shining a torch into my face.

I was never so pleased to see anyone in my life. I squirmed out from underneath her and searched among the stuffed animals till I found the cough linctus, and

then I poured some into the little plastic cup and gave it to her.

Then we lay side by side in the torchlight. From time to time Nani coughed.

"Can't understand what's given me this tickle, Yosser," she said, with a loud wheeze. "Just woke up with it. . ."

I didn't answer, but I felt my face get hot. I lay very still, thinking about the pin man's evil laughter and how he'd kept telling me to open the box. Then I pictured Nani's box, just a few metres away in my underwear drawer.

Supposing it really *did* contain a curse? Supposing it

contained the Deadly Curse of Samarkand?

Supposing *that* was why Nani didn't want it?

My imagination went into overdrive then. I thought about all the bad things that had happened lately – the recession, and the health and safety inspection, and Auntie Shabnam, and Sniper's gang, and the mallet – and suddenly it all made sense.

It was like a curse. And ever since Nani had spat on the puzzle box, everything *had* got worse.

I switched off the torch. Nani gave another wheeze, then turned over and hugged me. Gradually her breathing became slower, and she began to snore again.

I couldn't sleep, though. I just lay for hours in the darkness, holding onto Nani's nightie and wishing with all my heart that I'd left the box from Samarkand where it was.

Better out than in

The next morning, when Nani and me dragged ourselves downstairs, the first thing we saw was a large B&Q carrier bag lying on the breakfast table.

"Auntie Shabnam arrives on Monday," Mum said briskly. "That's just four days to convert her room into an ultra-smooth, ultra-chic executive office."

She took a roll of wallpaper out of the carrier bag and unfurled it. It had a design of red and gold zigzags.

"I thought we'd paint three walls Fiesta Red, with one jazzy Feature Wall," Mum went on. "Make a bit of a splash – what do you think?"

Nani cast a malevolent eye over the red and gold zigzags. With a grunt of extreme disapproval, followed by a wheeze, she poured milk over her cereal and the tablecloth, and the toast rack.

Frowning, Mum turned to me. "We can always paint over it with magnolia once Auntie Shabnam goes home," she said. "She'll like it, Yosser, won't she?"

I tried to imagine Nani's room as an ultra-smooth,

ultra-chic executive office with Fiesta Red walls and red and gold zigzags, but all I could think of was migraine headaches.

"It'll certainly be bold and contemporary," I said, and I glanced over at Nani, who was looking daggers at me.

"Might make the room look a bit small, though," I added.

Mum drained the last of her tea and walked over to the sink. Her shoulders, I noticed, were right down.

"It'll have to do," she said. "I don't have time to change it."

Then she took the carrier bag and headed upstairs. "I've only got the morning," she shouted back at us. "We're going to have another health and safety inspection, so the shop's got to be thoroughly cleaned."

Suddenly, I remembered Killer Queen. "No!" I shouted, jumping out of my chair. "Wait!" And I thundered up the stairs behind Mum, three at a time.

When I caught up with her, she had one hand on the bedroom door handle.

"It's OK, Mum," I said, pulling at the carrier bag. "You can go to the shop right now. Kylie and me'll do it."

Mum looked doubtful.

"Kylie's a dab hand at painting," I assured her. "We'll have the walls done by the time you and Dad get home – honest!"

I took out my mobile and texted Kylie, *Wanna hlp mk N's rm look lk a road axidnt*?

Within thirty seconds Kylie rang me back to say she was "well up for it". She also said she'd managed to get me a small portion of yesterday's tinned salmon for Killer Queen.

"Off you go," I told Mum. "It'll be fine. . ."

And, with a look of relief, and a dire warning not, on any account, to give Bilal a paintbrush, she hurried off.

***

Painting the walls – even Fiesta Red – was extremely soothing. Nani was downstairs entertaining Bilal, and so we'd put Killer Queen next door to sleep off her salmon-and-milk breakfast. For a while, we worked away in companionable silence.

Underneath the calm, though, everything was churning up inside me, and the more Nani's walls turned the colour of blood, the more they reminded me of the pin man, and Sniper's mallet, and my awful nightmare.

I could feel the tears at the back of my eyes, and every now and then they seemed to find their way down my nose, which made me sniff. Of course, it was only a matter of time before Kylie noticed.

"You OK, Yosser?" she asked.

I wanted more than anything to tell her why I was so upset, but I felt I shouldn't. The big birthday party was tomorrow night, after all. Her nerves must be stretched to breaking-point. So I said I was fine, and that I was only sniffing because of the paint.

"Have you noticed what a good view of your house you get from the window?" I said.

We stopped painting and went over to the window. Just then, Kylie's front door opened and her mum came out. She had on a backpack.

"She's off to the shops to buy in stuff for tomorrow," Kylie said. "There's a little 'do' in the house before the actual surprise party. She says I can sleep over with you,"

she added. "If that's OK?"

I nodded. "We can sleep in here in sleeping bags," I said. "With our backs to the Feature Wall. . ."

We watched Kylie's mum walk down the path. At the gate she paused, bent to examine a rose bush, then shook her head gravely.

"Greenfly," Kylie explained. "They're everywhere. Yesterday they decimated her early-flowering chrysanthemums."

"Can't she get greenfly spray?" I said. "That's what Nani uses on her pot plants. Mind you, you've got to stay well out of range when she's at it. . ."

Kylie shook her head. "Mum's strictly organic," she said. "No sprays, no slug pellets. She relies totally on ladybirds and frogs."

She sighed. "Nothing's going right for her at the moment. Nothing."

Sadly, we watched Kylie's mum disappear round the corner. Her back view reminded me of *my* mum's back view that morning.

"The noise was atrocious last night," Kylie went on. "The whole gang was in Sniper's room, and, honestly, you'd have thought the ceiling was going to cave in.

"Mum went up and asked him what was going on, and he just told her to keep her nose out of things that didn't concern her. That way, no one would get hurt."

She turned to me and said, in the saddest voice you could ever imagine, "I just want my mum to be happy, Yosser. And she isn't."

That did it. I couldn't hold back the tears any longer. All of a sudden they just spouted out of me and there I was, holding onto Kylie and weeping buckets and telling her all about the nightmare and the box and everything.

"I was going to give it to you for your mum," I sobbed. "But it's cursed, Kylie. *Cursed.* The pin man said so, and I know it sounds silly, but I believe him, 'cause *everything*'s going wrong for *everyone*. . ."

I was just drawing breath to launch into a list of all the things that had gone wrong since Nani spat on the box, when Kylie hissed, "Look!" and pointed, and there was Sniper, creeping out of the front door with a big bundle under his arm.

"I'll bet he's going to hide the murder weapon in the garden," Kylie whispered, "in case there's a police raid. That's what criminals always do. . ."

We watched Sniper flatten himself against the wall and creep round to the back of the house. When he got to the garden gate he dumped what he was carrying, looked around in all directions, stuck two fingers in his mouth and gave three sharp whistles.

"The signal," Kylie explained, and sure enough, in a couple of seconds Germane and Twista appeared and the three of them slapped one another's shoulders and banged one another's knuckles. Then, hooting and shrieking, they disappeared round the back, out of sight.

Sinking down onto the floor, Kylie wrung her hands in despair.

"It's like living with a time bomb," she said. "I just don't know where it'll all end."

Then she gave her head a shake, stood back up, and completely changed the subject. Kylie's great that way – she never lets things get her down for long.

"You've got to get a grip on this box thing, Yosser," she

said. "Curses only work because people believe in them. You read about them in books, but they aren't *real.*"

"But I *do* believe in the Curse of Samarkand," I said. "I've got it into my head, and even though I know it's stupid, I can't get it out."

"Exactly," said Kylie. "You've let your imagination get the better of you. There's only one thing to do," she said firmly. "Open the box. See for yourself there's nothing inside."

I thought about it, and the more I thought, the more I saw that Kylie was dead right.

"You've got to hunt for the key, Yosser," she went on. "Leave no stone unturned – it's got to be somewhere in the house."

Then she picked up her paintbrush and dipped it in the Fiesta Red paint tin.

"It's like my dad's always telling us," she said, as she ran a large red slash from one end of the wall to the other. "Things are better out than in. . ."

Germane

On Saturday morning I woke early, to the sound of pouring rain and Nani's wheezes.

There was a feeling of utter dread in my stomach, and a sour lump of guilt at the back of my throat.

I clambered carefully over Nani, fetched some milk from downstairs, then crept into the Fiesta Red bedroom. Killer Queen peeped out over the top of her box, and I lifted her out, and watched her drink the milk. Then I put her on my lap and stroked her.

Things couldn't have been much grimmer. That morning, Mum and Dad were going to paper the Feature Wall. On Monday morning the new furniture would arrive, and on Monday evening Auntie Shabnam would take up residence.

As far as Killer Queen was concerned, we'd reached the end of the road.

I held her against my cheek. Her fur was silk-soft and she smelled of fishy milk. "There's nowhere left for you to hide," I told her. "And I've no more food for you. And you're making Nani ill. I can't keep you. I just can't. . ."

Killer Queen meowed pathetically and watched, cross-eyed, as I gave her box a bit of a clean. Feeling incredibly sorry for myself, I lifted her back in, got dressed, and went downstairs to begin the hunt for the heart-shaped key.

I hunted everywhere. I climbed on chairs and ran my hands along every shelf. I tipped out every vase and every jar. I crawled under tables, searched inside drawers, and rummaged down the backs of settees and armchairs. I even felt inside the toes of ancient shoes and slippers. That key was *nowhere*.

By this time, things were beginning to stir upstairs. In double-quick time, I set the breakfast table, and by the time Mum and Dad appeared with Bilal, the tea was bubbling on the stove and the bread was in the toaster.

When everyone was settled round the table, I ran back upstairs and shifted Killer Queen into my bedroom. Kylie had given me a ball with a bell inside which belonged to one of the Papillons, and I threw it in the air and watched Killer Queen pounce on it, then roll onto her back and shred it with her back claws.

I wished I could play with her all morning, but of course I couldn't. Before you could say 'executive office', Mum and Dad and the wallpapering table were on their way up. I threw Killer Queen's ball one last time,

then went downstairs to keep Nani and Bilal company, and to take my mind off things.

All week, Nani had been playing a game with Bilal which involved a load of plastic tubs. Every time he put a small tub inside a bigger tub, Nani would say, "*In*, Bilal. Say *in*," and every time he tipped one out, she would say "*Out*, Bilal. Say *out*."

The game was incredibly tedious, and Bilal only ever made gurgling noises, but Nani kept on and on at it. I suspected anything was better than thinking about red and gold zigzags and Auntie Shabnam. I sat on the settee beside Nani and we watched Bilal.

"Any progress?" I asked.

Nani smiled and shook her head. "The best things in life," she said solemnly, "take time. *Out,* Bilal."

I sat for a bit, watching Bilal dribble into his tubs. Then, cautiously, I said, "You know the key for the puzzle box, Nani? I don't suppose you have any idea. . .?"

Nani frowned and chewed the inside of her cheek. Then she shook her head.

"If you don't mind," I went on, "I'd like to give the box to Kylie's mum for her fortieth birthday."

To my relief, Nani's face softened a little. "Go ahead, Yosser," she said. "And I hope it brings her more joy than it brought *me*. *In*, Bilal."

***

By lunchtime I'd had more than enough of the *In/Out* game, so I changed into my very best jeans and my turquoise-and-silver kameez, and my glitziest turquoise hijab. I found an umbrella, and went to Kylie's house to see if she needed help with the 'do'.

When Kylie opened the door, she looked completely stressed out. Her hair was sticking straight up, and there were streaks of purple glittery stuff on it, and on her arms and her face.

She had two Papillons clamped to her chest. Another two were running in and out between her legs. Behind her, three more leapt up and down like demented jack-in-the-boxes. Every single dog was barking fit to burst.

"We usually keep the Papillons in the dining room," Kylie explained, "but we've set out the buffet there. Can't trust them with a roomful of canapés. . ." And she handed one to me.

Now, I'll be honest, I'm not that keen on Papillons. I know they're very cute, with their shiny black noses and their funny butterfly ears and everything, and I could probably cope with *one* if it was reasonably calm – but seven hysterical Papillons was *way* too much for me. And, that afternoon, it was definitely too much for Kylie as well.

I dumped my umbrella and tried to sidle in, but my way was completely blocked. Then, as I turned to close the door, a Papillon took hold of the hem of my jeans – my *very best* jeans – and proceeded to shake it vigorously from side to side.

Handing me another Papillon, Kylie tried to pull the jean-ripper off. Immediately, the three jack-in-the-boxes smelt freedom and flew out of the door and down the garden path. With an agonised cry, Kylie raced after them.

As soon as she'd gone, the remaining Papillon joined forces with its friend, and a spirited tug-of-war began.

I watched in horror as my very best jeans *ever* were shredded before my eyes. Then, when it seemed things couldn't possibly get any worse, they did. Germane arrived.

Taking gigantic strides that sent all the Papillons flying, he strode up the path towards me, and as he walked he slowly drew his hand out of his pocket. I saw the bright flash of something small and silver.

A knife? A razor blade?

On the doorstop, Germane bent so that his face was level with mine. This close, he was simply enormous, and he was wearing some sort of musky stuff that made me feel quite lightheaded.

I gazed, mesmerised, into his shades. Every sequin of my glitzy turquoise hijab was reflected there. So were the whites of my eyes.

Above the shades, Germane's dreadlocks hung like wet creepers in a dusky-grey forest, and somewhere to the left of his nose, a diamond sparkled like a solitary star in a dark, dark sky. For a long time, neither of us spoke. Then Germane did.

"You Yosser Farooq, then?" he said, in a big, deep voice.

For a split second I considered denying it. Then I nodded. I was beyond terrified.

"Got somefink for ya, Yosser Farooq," Germane said,

and he opened his hand, and held the silver object right under my nose.

I looked down into his massive palm. All I could make out through the rain was a vague silver shape which was pointed at one end. Desperately, I stood on tiptoe and tried to catch Kylie's eye but Kylie, oblivious to my plight, was still chasing Papillons.

I was all on my own with Germane and a deadly weapon. The Curse of Samarkand had struck again.

Discovered

You know that feeling when you're *so* embarrassed, you wish a wormhole would open under your feet and suck you into a parallel universe?

That was the feeling I got when I finally realised what was in Germane's hand.

I'm still not sure of the exact sequence of events, because afterwards I reckon I was in post-traumatic shock, but I *think* I must have said something like, "Please, *please,* put that away. Please."

It must have been something like that, because then Germane said, "No way, sister. Dis here has cost me a lorra bovver, know wot I mean?" And he pressed the silver thing into my hand.

Which is when I began to think I might, just *might*, have got it wrong. . .

The silver thing didn't feel like a knife or a razor blade. It was soft and warm. It also had a faintly meaty smell – though, in fairness to me, the meaty smell was pretty hard to make out, on account of Germane's overpoweringly musky one.

The actual moment of realisation came when Germane said, "Chicken livers, innit. For da pussy-cat."

That was when I wished the wormhole would open. *That* was when I wished I'd never been born.

Fortunately, at that precise moment a swarming, squealing stream of wet white fur rushed towards us. Germane made his escape into the house, leaving me standing on the doorstep, gazing down at the river of Papillons.

"Stop *chatting,* Yosser!" Kylie shouted on her way past. "The fruit punch isn't even started!"

I shoved the foil parcel of chicken livers into my pocket and followed Kylie into the kitchen. I must have looked like a zombie. I certainly felt like one.

Tersely, Kylie handed me an apple and a knife. Then she opened a carton of blackcurrant cordial and poured it into a bowl.

"Twista's been upstairs banging and thumping with Sniper since first light," she muttered. "And now Germane's arrived. Who knows what they're up to?"

She poured in a second carton. Her hand was shaking.

"As if that wasn't enough," she went on, "now Mum says we've to use my bedroom for the coats and umbrellas.

I'm dead scared someone's going to step on Toffee 'n' Caramel. . ."

I stared miserably into the bowl of blood-red cordial. Another vision of the man with the pins and the woman with the puzzle box flashed through my mind. This time, the vision was accompanied by the agonised screams of mortally-injured Russian Dwarf hamsters. I badly wanted to cry.

"It's 'cause we're cursed, Kylie," I said. "Everything – *everything* – goes wrong for us."

Kylie ran her hands through her glittery hair. Then she gave me a long, hard look.

"You need to open that box, Yosser," she said. "You need to see for yourself it's not got a curse inside."

She put down the empty carton. "We're getting out of here," she said decisively. "We'll finish making the punch, then take Toffee 'n' Caramel and Castle Hamster to your nani's bedroom, out of harm's way. We'll keep watch on Sniper from the window, and then I'll help you look for the key.

"*Not*, you understand," she added, "that I believe in the Deadly Curse of Samarkand. The Deadly Curse of Samarkand is merely a psychological phenomenon with which you have become obsessed. You do *realise* that, don't you?"

I nodded meekly and, as the two of us chopped

up apples, I concentrated hard on thinking of the Deadly Curse of Samarkand as a psychological phenomenon with which I had become obsessed.

I had to admit it made me feel ever so slightly better.

When the punch was all ready for Kylie's mum to add the vodka, Kylie and me crept upstairs. We gathered up Toffee 'n' Caramel, and all their personal effects, ready for the Great Escape.

"We needn't take the tubes or the yoghurt pots," Kylie said, as she pushed Castle Hamster up under her T-shirt. "It's important to look as inconspicuous as possible."

I looked at Toffee 'n' Caramel's cage, which was an enormous plastic thing with built-in exercise wheels, and decided there was no way I could carry it inconspicuously. So I slipped a hamster gently into each of my

jeans pockets, added a sprinkling of sunflower seeds, and followed Kylie out onto the landing.

We were just about to go downstairs when the doorbell rang and Kylie's mum, in a gold sparkly catsuit, ran down the hall, threw the door open, and ushered in my mum. Mum had Bilal in one hand and an umbrella and a shiny box in the other.

"Quick!" hissed Kylie, reversing. "Hide!"

We heard Kylie's mum telling my mum to slip off her wet shawl and make herself at home. Then we heard her coming upstairs with the shawl and the umbrella. With great difficulty, we shuffled along the landing. Outside Sniper's room, we flattened ourselves against the wall as inconspicuously as possible.

When Kylie's mum got to the top of the stairs she stopped, and for a moment I was sure she'd seen us. Kylie obviously thought so too, because she pressed herself right up against me. Her body was absolutely rigid, and I tried hard to make mine rigid too.

Then a hamster began to wriggle about in one of my pockets. That made it harder than ever to stay still, particularly when I thought about the effect a mixture of sunflower husks, chicken liver and hamster poo might be having on my best jeans.

At last Kylie's mum went into Kylie's room, and we relaxed against the wall. And that was when we heard Twista.

"When're you gettin' rid of the old woman then, Sniper?" he said.

"Cool it, man," Sniper replied. "She'll be gone soon enough. Can't do nothin', anyhow, till it's dark."

Then we heard Germane's low, gravelly voice. "Need to get rid of your kid sister an' all," he said. "Don't want her squealin', now, do we?"

"It's OK, man," Sniper assured him. "Gorra sleepover wif her pal, innit."

At that moment, Kylie's mum came back out. To our relief, she went straight downstairs.

"Quick!" hissed Kylie. "Let's get out while we still can!" And we tore down the stairs and out into the rain – which by now was torrential.

When we got to my house we were absolutely soaked. A lot of the pink paint from Castle Hamster had dissolved onto Kylie's T-shirt, and most of the purple glitter from her hair had washed down to join it. My jeans were plastered to my skin, and there was a horrible stickiness running down my legs. I dreaded to think how Toffee 'n' Caramel must be feeling.

"You can use the bathroom first," I told Kylie as I led the way upstairs. Then, without thinking, I threw myself against my bedroom door, fell inside . . . and almost died of shock.

Sitting on the bed, in a white-and-silver sari, with the most beautiful white lace dupatta on her head, was Nani.

On her lap, sleeping peacefully, lay Killer Queen.

Secrets

Smiling, Nani held up a small white plastic bottle.

"Antihistamines," she said, with a wink. "But if you'd told me sooner, I wouldn't have had *any* wheezes. . ."

I swallowed hard. "I'm sorry, Nani-jee," I said. "*Abjectly* sorry."

Then, being careful not to wake Killer Queen, I reached into my pockets, felt stickily around, and grasped Toffee in one hand and Caramel in the other.

"They're Kylie's," I explained, holding them out for Nani to see. "And they're only staying the night – honest."

Nani pushed her spectacles up onto her forehead and examined each hamster in turn.

"Good for you, Yosser," she said, replacing the spectacles. "So now we have no more secrets from one another. Mmm?" And she patted the bed.

I put Toffee 'n' Caramel back, and sat down. I wasn't quite sure what Nani meant about the 'secrets', but I was suddenly very aware of the box from Samarkand lying hidden in my underwear drawer.

"*I* don't have any more secrets, Nani," I said. "Have *you*?"

For a while Nani sat in silence, stroking Killer Queen. Then, putting her into my lap, she clambered up onto the bed and lifted down the wildcat from beside Smartypants' bowl. Smartypants immediately perked right up.

Nani sat back down beside me with the wildcat balanced across her knees. This close, it looked positively evil. Its stripy brown fur stood right up on end, and its golden glass eyes stared menacingly. Its back was arched and its mouth gaped open in a great frozen snarl. I prayed Killer Queen wouldn't wake up and see it.

"This came from Samarkand," Nani said.

"Along with the box?" I asked.

Nani nodded. "Bit of a job lot, you might say," and she ran her hand thoughtfully along the bristly arch of the wildcat's back.

"So the person who gave you the wildcat," I said, choosing my words carefully, "also gave you the beautiful box?"

Nani nodded again.

Water was gurgling in the bathroom, and I knew if I didn't find out Nani's secret now, the chance might never come again. With my nani, timing is everything.

"Was the person Nana?" I asked, and, sighing, Nani shook her head.

"Your nana didn't hold with killing, Yosser," she whispered. "No, these gifts were given to me a long, long time ago. When I was very, very young, and rather . . . impressionable. . ."

I could feel Killer Queen stretching. I could also hear the bathroom door opening.

"Was he very handsome?" I whispered, and I bit my lip and waited for Nani's answer.

The answer never came, though, because at that moment Kylie burst in with a towel round her head, saw the wildcat on Nani's lap, and screamed. That woke Killer Queen, and then Killer Queen saw the wildcat too, and *she* gave a squeal, leapt several metres into the air, and was caught by Kylie seconds before she hit the floor.

Then Toffee (or Caramel) decided that conditions in my pocket had finally become unbearable and darted out and disappeared under the bed, and Nani, in an attempt to stop him, jumped up and dropped the wildcat on my foot. There was a dull *snap* as a hind leg split, and a little stream of sawdust ran out onto the carpet.

For what seemed like forever, Kylie and Nani and me stood looking at one another, and then, quite suddenly, Nani put her arms round us both, took an enormous breath in, and said:

"You know what I think? I think you two should catch all the animals and put them somewhere where they won't eat one another, and then clean yourselves up, and put on some party gear, and get along to Kylie's house pronto – because we are currently missing a great 'do'!"

And that is exactly what we did. Which is why I'll probably never know if Nani's man from Samarkand *was* very handsome. But, judging by the look in her eyes before she dropped the wildcat, I kind of guess he was. . .

***

Strangely enough, Kylie and me quite enjoyed the 'do'. To start with, anyway.

We caught Toffee (or Caramel), and then I had a shower and got changed in lightning-quick time. I gave Kylie my pink sparkly salwar kameez to wear, and she said it made her feel like a princess, and I wore my all-time favourite midnight-blue one, with the diamond-trimmed hijab.

The 'do' went on all afternoon. There was lots of food and balloons and dancing and games, and Kylie's mum had a great time blowing out candles and unwrapping presents and telling people they shouldn't have.

Bilal had a ball too. He'd never met the Papillons before, and he quickly discovered that if there's one thing better than a Papillon, it's *seven* Papillons, especially when they jump all over you and lick your face.

All in all, it couldn't have gone better. Until the conga, that is. That was when things deteriorated, big-style.

Kylie's dad started it. Holding a large silver bag, he jumped up on the table and blew several shrill blasts on his party hooter. When everyone was quiet, he pulled out a red velvet devil's costume, and a hairband with two red velvet horns that wobbled about on wires.

"Get changed, love," he said, throwing the costume over to Kylie's mum. "Taxis'll be here in half an hour to whisk us off to the Masons' Arms for the *real* 'do'! But before we go. . ." he wiggled his hips and snapped imaginary castanets, ". . .let's *conga*!"

Everyone cheered, and Kylie's mum hugged the devil's costume to her chest and said she'd honestly had no idea. Then we all made a chain with Kylie's mum wearing the red velvet horns at the front, and me and Kylie, with Bilal sandwiched between us, at the back. (Nani decided a conga would play havoc with her rheumatics, so she sat on the settee and banged out the beat on the cream crackers tin.)

It was when we were conga-ing round the dining room table that Kylie suddenly gave my waist a sharp squeeze.

"Look, Yosser," she hissed. "Over by the cheese-and-pineapple sticks. . ."

I looked, and there were Sniper and Twista leaning against the table, stuffing their pockets with potato crisps and vol-au-vents.

"See the way they keep pointing at Mum and laughing?" Kylie went on. "I'm telling you, Yosser – the minute everyone leaves for the Masons' Arms, all hell's going to break loose."

She let go of the person in front and ran out into the hall, pulling me and Bilal with her.

"Those . . . social misfits. . ." she spluttered. "They've got absolutely no consideration for other people. Let's go back to your house," she went on, her voice smouldering with rage. "I can't bear to breathe the same *air*. . ." And she ran out into the rain.

I didn't want Bilal getting soaked (*or* my midnight-blue salwar kameez, for that matter) so I dashed upstairs to get an umbrella. I was halfway up, when suddenly the whole world went black.

For a moment I could see nothing. Then I smelt the unmistakable scent of musk, and realised my way was blocked by Germane. Next thing, he sat down on the stairs above me, took off his shades and smiled down at me. One of his teeth had a golden star, right in the middle.

"Yo, sister!" he said, with a whistle. "You sure is lookin' like a little Killer Queen!"

Then he threw back his big head and laughed, and his laughter was like big, soft, velvety rumbles.

Birthday Surprises

The night of Kylie's mum's surprise party was the wettest, most miserable night of my life.

All evening Kylie put a brave face on it, but you could tell she was in a terrible mood, and even Mum's pizzas – with no fewer than *twelve* different toppings – didn't cheer her up as much as you'd think.

After tea, Kylie and me went up to the Fiesta Red room, which I'd made as cosy as possible for the sleepover. I'd moved in our sleeping bags and my make-up mirror and every item of make-up and nail polish I possessed, because I'd promised Kylie a radical Face 'n' Nail Makeover to cheer her up.

I'd also moved in the wildcat, because I didn't want Nani breathing in sawdust, and I'd propped it up against Castle Hamster. And, finally, I'd taken the dreaded puzzle box out of my underwear drawer, and laid it on Kylie's sleeping bag.

When we were all nicely settled, I picked up the box, positioned my fingers on the three pearl petals, and

demonstrated how to get the sides to spring out and show the heart-shaped hole. Then I handed the box to Kylie, and she examined it from all angles.

When she'd finished, she said, "It's fabulous, thank you, even if it doesn't open." She said it in rather a flat voice, though, and I could see that, like me, she had very mixed feelings about it.

"We could sneak downstairs when the grown-ups are in bed," I suggested, "and have a final, all-out search for the key. Two heads are better than one. . ."

But in the end we didn't. I guess we'd both decided it was a lost cause. Instead, we took turns playing with Toffee 'n' Caramel and Killer Queen, and I tried hard not to think about what Mum and Dad were going to say when – inevitably – they found out about her. Then, when Nani came up to bed, I started Kylie's makeover.

But Kylie's heart wasn't really in it. Every fifteen minutes or so, I had to stop to let her go and peer out of the window, and every time she did, her mood darkened. After one particularly bad session, when she said she'd distinctly seen Germane with the mallet, I braced myself.

"Perhaps," I said, carefully sticking a plastic ruby in the middle of her thumbnail, "we've got it wrong about Sniper and his gang. . ."

Kylie looked at me as though I'd gone completely mad. "What's to get wrong?" she asked sharply.

"Sniper and his gang are the very Embodiment of Evil. There's no two ways about it."

I bit my tongue. There was, after all, no doubt that Sniper and Twista were pretty challenged in the social skills department, but as for Germane . . . I wasn't at all sure any more.

Ever since he'd given me the chicken livers, I'd been wondering, and that afternoon, when he'd smiled his starry smile at me and told me I was "lookin' like a little Killer Queen", I really thought Kylie and me might have got hold of the wrong end of the stick.

I didn't like to say it outright, though – not with the way Kylie was feeling. It seemed somehow disloyal. Next morning, however, when the sun rose brightly on Kylie's mum's fortieth birthday, I was proved right. We *had* got hold of the wrong end of the stick.

In fact, we'd got hold of the wrong *stick*.

***

We were woken very early by Bilal banging us on the head with a plastic tub and shouting "Ow! Ow! Ow!" at the top of his voice.

"Is he still teething?" Kylie muttered sleepily. "Sounds like he's in agony. . ."

I'd just opened my mouth to explain about the *In/Out*

game, when several things happened in rapid succession.

First, Kylie's mobile gave a muffled ring from somewhere under the sleeping bags, and she jerked the sleeping bag up, catching the corner of Castle Hamster, which tipped over.

Next, an extremely dishevelled Toffee 'n' Caramel appeared through the portcullis, and Bilal, with a scream of delight, made a nose-dive in their direction. The nose-dive dislodged the wildcat, which tipped over onto its side.

Then Kylie yelled "*Mum*!" and Bilal yelled "*Out*!" at exactly the same time, and there on the carpet, beside the wildcat's gaping jaws, lay a tiny, heart-shaped key.

Quick as a flash Bilal pounced, picked the heart up, sniffed it, and licked his lips. Then, with a loud, and very definite, "*In*", he put it into his mouth.

I have never moved so fast in all my life. I lunged across the sleeping bag at Bilal, forced his lips open, and grabbed the heart just before it disappeared down his throat. Then I wiped him down, and held the heart up for Kylie to see.

But Kylie had other things on her mind. She was pulling on her jeans and heading for the door.

"Mum's *hysterical*!" she yelled back at me. "Something *catastrophic* has happened!"

My stomach did a back-flip. Pausing only to deposit a howling Bilal on Nani's bed, I followed Kylie.

"What's happened?" I asked her as we ran. "What did your mum say?"

"She was *incoherent*," Kylie told me breathlessly. "Said something about 'that Sniper of mine' . . . and 'you'll never guess what 'im and 'is mates've gone and done. . . ' She kept sobbing, Yosser," she said, finally. "Sobbing fit to burst. . ."

It was like a waking nightmare. I just couldn't take it in. All the way to Kylie's house, the most awful images ran round and round in my head.

I saw Germane, holding his mallet aloft and singing the all-too-familiar words, "Bang-bang-bang, an' it'll knock 'em dead!" Then, as I followed Kylie up the garden path, he stopped being Germane and morphed into the man with the pins.

And the man with the pins had the puzzle box – *Nani*'s puzzle box – in one hand, and the little wooden heart in the other, and he was opening it, and out was flying the Deadly Curse of Samarkand. And even though I still didn't know what the Deadly Curse of Samarkand actually was, I was suddenly *convinced* I was about to see it in Kylie's back garden.

I must have put my hands over my eyes, because all I remember as we went through the gate was hearing lots of barking, and voices singing Happy Birthday, and then a loud cheer and a *pop!* Then I felt Kylie pulling at my hands, and screaming, "It's OK, Yosser! It's OK! You can look!"

And when I did, I honestly, *honestly*, didn't know whether to laugh or cry.

There, in the middle of the cabbage patch, stood a small, very rickety building made out of long sticks, string and corrugated plastic. It was covered in red heart-shaped balloons, and there was a banner draped across it that said, 'Happy 40th Brithday, Mum', in big red letters.

The plastic door was open, and inside you could see wooden shelves supported by empty lager cans. The shelves were stacked high with plant pots and bags of potting compost, and there was a fork, and a trowel, and a pair of cutters, all with pink flowery handles.

On one side of the building, in floods of tears, stood Kylie's mum, and a very embarrassed Sniper. On the other side stood Kylie's dad, towered over by Germane and Twista. Germane was holding a foaming bottle of champagne.

When she saw us, Kylie's mum gave a big sniff and said, "Come on, boys – do your Birthday Rap again for Kylie and Yosser!" and Sniper and Twista and Germane cleared away the Papillons, stood in a line, and, with appropriate movements, they sang:

"If you wanna grow a cabbage or a brussel sprout,
Then you gorra keep the heat in and the greenflies out. . .
So dis 'ere is da way to make your veg'tables grow good –
It's da coolest little hothouse in da neighbourhood – Yay!"

When they had finished, Kylie's mum gave each of them a big kiss, and said it was the happiest day of her entire life. Then Kylie's dad went and got the camera and took a photo of us all.

Kylie stood beside Sniper for the photo, and I stood on tiptoe between Germane and Twista, and I honestly thought I would *burst* with happiness.

Auntie Shabnam

The next day we all went to the airport to collect Auntie Shabnam, and by the time we'd squeezed ourselves and three big bouquets of flowers into the car, there was hardly room to breathe.

On the journey, we were all a bit subdued. Nani sat beside me in the back with Bilal on her knee, watching him stick his thumb in his mouth and say "*In*", then take it back out and say "*Out*". But we hardly spoke.

Now that the big day had finally come, I was nervous as anything. I kept wondering what Auntie Shabnam would be like, and whether she'd really be able to help with the business, and – most of all – whether we'd get on.

I also wondered whether she would approve of her office, which now sported a smoked-glass desk, a state-of-the-art computer, and a day-bed covered in scarlet silk cushions and a deep brown faux-fur throw.

It also sported the wildcat, because we'd fixed its leg and asked Nani if we could have it, and Nani had given a sniff and said that we were welcome. In fact, she'd added, Auntie Shabnam could take it back to Lahore with her, for all *she* cared.

So we put it on the shelf above the computer, and it looked great with the faux-fur throw.

As for the puzzle box – after the birthday breakfast, Kylie and me finally opened it and (surprise, surprise!) there was no Deadly Curse of Samarkand inside.

There was *something* inside, though. Something even more beautiful than the box itself. I put it in an envelope, and I put the envelope into my underwear drawer till the time was right to give it back to Nani, and I kept thinking about it.

And the more I thought about it, and about the man who'd shot the wildcat, the more I understood why Nani didn't like the box from Samarkand. . .

***

The Lahore flight took forever to arrive, and the longer it took, the more nervous I felt. I kept thinking how incredibly clever and high-powered Auntie Shabnam was, and worrying that she might find *us* a bit dull.

I also suspected she'd be quite glamorous, because Mum had shown me photos of her, and sometimes incredibly glamorous people can be a bit difficult to cope with.

But I needn't have worried. The minute Auntie Shabnam appeared in the Arrivals Hall, the 'Auntie Shabnam Worry Factor' plummeted to zero. She was seriously *cool*!

She had short black hair, long sparkling earrings and the sunniest smile I'd ever seen, and she was wearing a grey leather jacket, black leather trousers and high-heeled red boots. As soon as she saw us, she made a bee-line for me and gave me a great big hug.

"State-of-the-art jeans, Yosser," she said, handing me a carrier bag with 'Dubai' written on it. "I hope you like them!"

I had a quick peek and boy, did I *ever*! Then we all squeezed into the car, and Bilal showed Auntie Shabnam his *In/Out* trick all the way home, and she said he was brilliant, and probably a businessman in the making.

Then we settled her into her office, which she said was 'just the job' and, after a special meal, the grown-ups sat down to talk Business Plans.

It all sounded great, especially the interactive website which Auntie Shabnam said would "rocket Farooq's Fruits into the twenty-first century", but it had been a long day, and when they got to the health and safety issue I said I thought I'd turn in.

I didn't get far, though. As I stood up to go, Nani's foot clamped down heavily on top of mine, and she wiggled her eyebrows meaningfully. I sat back down.

"As I see it," Auntie Shabnam was saying, "the hygiene issue is paramount. We at Farooq's Fruits must employ the very latest in antiseptics, anti-bacterials, and hi-tech anti-vermin devices. . ."

She paused and looked over at Nani. "And to that end," she went on, "I believe Auntie here has a suggestion."

Nani cleared her throat. "Auntie has indeed," she said. "It's the very latest in Vermin Control and it's called

Killer Queen. It's not too hi-tech yet," she went on, "but give it a couple of months and it'll be *lethal*."

She turned to me. "Perhaps, Yosser," she said, "you would be so kind as to fetch it?"

I could see Mum and Dad were trying hard to keep their faces straight, and as I closed the door I heard a lot of laughter, so I reckoned Nani had already prepared the ground, but still, I said a little prayer as I presented Killer Queen to the committee.

I needn't have worried, though. They passed her unanimously, and they decided she would stay in the house for the next few weeks, then take up residence in the shop. Which, though not ideal, was a million times better than losing her entirely.

***

Later that night, when Nani came to bed, I handed her the envelope.

"It's a ring," I said. "It was in the box from Samarkand."

Nani looked at the ring for ages. I waited for her to say something, but she didn't, and perhaps it was just as well. Perhaps some things are better kept secret.

Then, all of a sudden, she brightened right up. She took my hand, winked at me, then slipped the gold ring onto

my finger. It fitted exactly. I couldn't believe it. I'd never had such a precious thing, ever.

"Thank you, Nani-jee," I said. "It's perfect."

Nani gave me a big hug.

"You're welcome, Yosser," she said. "And I hope it brings you good fortune."

Then we settled down to sleep, and as I lay there next to Nani with the Golden Ring from Samarkand on my finger, I realised that, finally, everything was as perfect as it could possibly be.

And you know what? I wasn't beset by one single, solitary worry.

Not one.

Franzeska G. Ewart

I've written over 25 books for children, and I also write for adults. I live in the village of Lochwinnoch, in Scotland, where I enjoy the countryside and wildlife.

For me, writing a children's book always involves the same processes. Here they are. . .

First, there's THINKING – what will I write about? I find it helps to look at pictures, and books, and the internet. It also helps to *move*. My best ideas come when I'm walking or cycling.

I got the idea for *There's a Hamster in my Pocket!* from a puzzle box I saw on YouTube. It seemed just the sort of thing Nani would have!

Then, there's RESEARCHING – finding things out. For *There's a Hamster in my Pocket!* I had to find out about puzzle boxes and Papillons. And I also had to watch bits of a really *horrible* film. . .!

Next, I decide on CHARACTERS. For *There's a Hamster in my Pocket!* the new characters were Sniper, Twista and Germane.

I always draw my characters before I write about them, because it helps bring them to life.

Finally, I do a CHAPTER PLAN (that can be tricky!) and then I can get down to the actual WRITING. And *that* is the best part of all!

Writing can be a lonely business but, as you can see, my two cats – Lily and her son The Woozle – are with me every step of the way!

Read more about Yosser and Kylie's adventures in
Sita, Snake Queen of Speed
by Franzeska G. Ewart

When Yosser's best friend, Kylie, comes back from Thrill City she is full of amazing stories about the best ride there – Sita, Snake-Queen of Speed! Yosser knows that she MUST go on the ride . . . but how? An opportunity presents itself when Kylie's dad's prize ferret, Thunderball Silver the Third, mysteriously goes missing just days before the Grand Ferret Championships. Will Yosser and Kylie find a way to catch the ferret-thief and earn enough money to make their dreams come true?

"A simple story of friendship."
Kirkus Reviews

Praise for Franzeska G. Ewart:
"Sensitive and funny."
The Guardian